"I'm Going to Kill Her!"

"I'm absolutely positively going to kill her," Elizabeth seethed.

"Good. She deserves it," Amy said. "She's making things worse and worse! First she steals your baby-sitting job, and then she sticks you with the worst possible booth in the entire fair!"

Elizabeth just kept shaking her head. "My very own sister. How could she do this to me?" Jessica had gotten her into difficult situations before, but this one had to be the worst.

"I'm going to find her right now," Elizabeth said furiously. "I'm not kidding, Amy. There's no way that Jessica's going to get away with this!"

SWEET VALLEY TWINS

Jessica and the Brat Attack

Written by
Jamie Suzanne

Created by
FRANCINE PASCAL

A BANTAM SKYLARK BOOK®
NEW YORK · TORONTO · LONDON · SYDNEY · AUCKLAND

RL 4, 008-012

JESSICA AND THE BRAT ATTACK
A Bantam Skylark Book / May 1989

Conceived by Francine Pascal

*Produced by Daniel Weiss Associates, Inc.,
27 West 20th Street,
New York, NY 10011*

Cover art by James Mathewuse.

ISBN 0-553-15695-0

Published simultaneously in the United States and Canada

Bantam Books are published by Bantam Books, a division of Bantam
Doubleday Dell Publishing Group, Inc. Its trademark, consisting of
the words "Bantam Books" and the portrayal of a rooster, is Registered
in U.S. Patent and Trademark Office and in other countries. Marca
Registrada. Bantam Books, 666 Fifth Avenue, New York, New York 10103.

PRINTED IN THE UNITED STATES OF AMERICA

O   0 9 8 7 6 5 4 3 2

To
Jaclyn Moritz

One

◇

"I can't wait for the sixth-grade fair!" Lila Fowler exclaimed excitedly. She set her tray down on the lunch table and slid into a chair next to Jessica Wakefield. Everyone at the table was talking about the fair, which the sixth graders at Sweet Valley Middle School were having on Saturday to raise money for future class trips.

Jessica's blue-green eyes sparkled. "It's going to be great. I hope I get to be in charge of the Wheel of Fortune."

Julie Porter, one of the organizers of the fair, shook her head. Julie was in charge of giving out assignments to the students who would be running booths. "Don't forget, Jessica. We have to pick numbers out of a hat to find out who's going to be in charge of what booth. Don't get your heart set on one particular booth."

"Right." Lila giggled. "You might get stuck with the water-balloon toss!"

Jessica wrinkled her nose. Everyone knew the water-balloon toss was the one bad booth out of the ten. Jessica certainly didn't want a bunch of kids throwing wet balloons at her.

"Did I hear someone mention water balloons?" Elizabeth Wakefield asked, coming over with her tray.

Julie Porter gave her a big smile. She and Elizabeth worked together on *The Sweet Valley Sixers*, the sixth-grade newspaper, and they were good friends. "I was just telling your double not to get her hopes up about Saturday. We'll be picking booth assignments out of a hat after school today. Till then, no one knows who's going to get what."

"I hope there aren't too many people interested in running booths," Lila commented. "There aren't very many good ones to go around."

"Well, I won't be your competition," Elizabeth said. "I'm helping Olivia Davidson design posters instead."

Jessica sighed dramatically. "Can you believe we're sisters?" she said to no one in particular. "Who'd want to sit around designing boring posters when you could be doing something exciting like running a booth?"

Elizabeth smiled. In spite of the fact that she

and Jessica were identical twins, they were almost complete opposites. They looked exactly alike, with their long blond hair, blue-green eyes, and tiny dimples in their left cheeks, but their personalities were as different as night and day.

Jessica loved being the center of attention. She was a member of the Boosters, the middle school's cheerleading squad. She was also a member of the Unicorn Club, an exclusive group made up of the most popular girls in school, including her friends Lila Fowler and Ellen Riteman. Jessica loved having a good time more than anything, and sometimes she had trouble taking her schoolwork seriously.

Elizabeth was the exact opposite. She loved school, she loved to read, and she hoped to be a writer one day. Her best friends, Amy Sutton and Julie Porter, both worked on the sixth-grade newspaper with her, and all three of them thought that members of the Unicorn Club were silly and stuck-up. In fact, they often referred to them as the "Snob Squad."

"I hope we raise lots of money from the fair," Lila said, taking a bite of her ice cream sandwich. "Then maybe we'll get to take a really good class trip, like to Paris or something."

Everyone laughed at once. Lila came from one of the wealthier families in Sweet Valley and she was extremely spoiled. She never had to ask for anything more than once, and she had already been to Europe several times.

"No way, Lila," Julie said, groaning. "We'll be lucky to raise enough money to take a trip to San Diego!"

Lila frowned. "You never know," she said airily. "If you don't set your sights high, you'll never get anywhere at all. That's what my dad always says."

Only Jessica seemed to agree. "Lila's right," she said loyally. "I hope we raise enough money to go somewhere really glamorous."

Elizabeth unwrapped her tuna sandwich and took a bite. "Where is the drawing to see who gets which booth?" she asked curiously. Even though she herself wouldn't be in charge of a booth, she couldn't wait to hear who'd have each job.

"In Mr. Bowman's classroom, right after school today," Julie said. She turned to Jessica and Lila and added, "Make sure everyone who wants to be in charge of a booth shows up."

"I can't wait to do the Wheel of Fortune," Jessica exclaimed. "I've got the perfect outfit ready for it!"

Elizabeth had to hide a smile. When Jessica got excited about something, there was no point in trying to tell her not to get her hopes up!

*   *   *

Elizabeth went out to the lawn to meet her best friend, Amy Sutton, when she was finished eating lunch. Amy was sitting on the ground with her legs drawn up, resting her chin on her knees.

"What's the matter? You look upset," Elizabeth said, plopping down beside her on the grass.

"I am, a little," Amy admitted. "I've got to baby-sit for Mrs. Sampson this Saturday. When I agreed to do it, I completely forgot about the fair. That means I can't be in charge of a booth."

"Oh, that's too bad," Elizabeth said sympathetically. She knew how much her friend had been looking forward to the fair.

"If it were anyone else I'd try to get out of it. But I promised her a long time ago, and she pays really well. Anyway, she'd have a hard time finding someone else on such short notice," Amy said.

Elizabeth was quiet for a minute. "Maybe you could find someone to take your place."

Amy shook her head. "Who's going to want to work on the day of the fair? Everyone wants to be at the park." She sighed.

Elizabeth patted her friend on the arm. "Cheer up," she said brightly. "How about if I take over for you?"

Amy stared at her. "Why? Don't you want to go to the fair?"

"Well," Elizabeth explained, "I'm not planning on running a booth or anything, so it wouldn't be that big a deal for me to miss it. What time are you supposed to baby-sit?"

"From ten to five," Amy said.

"So I could go to the fair for a little while in the morning."

Amy's eyes lit up. "You're the best friend in the entire world," she cried. "Can I really tell Mrs. Sampson you'll take my place?"

"Sure," Elizabeth said, grinning. "But you'd better coach me so I know what to do."

"Oh, don't worry about it," Amy reassured her. "Mrs. Sampson said there'll just be the two youngest ones at home on Saturday."

Elizabeth raised her eyebrows. "Just the two youngest? How many are there all together?"

"Four," Amy said with a groan. "You're lucky the older two won't be there. They're monsters. Anyway, I wouldn't worry," she went on. "The worst they can do is tie you to a chair and try to cut off all your hair. That's what they did to me once."

Elizabeth's hands flew to her blond ponytail and Amy doubled up, laughing.

"You can still back out of it," she offered.

But Elizabeth shook her head. "I'm brave,"

she declared. "If you've managed to survive the monsters, I guess I can, too!"

After school that day, Mr. Bowman picked up the straw hat on his desk and looked at the sixth graders who had signed up to be in charge of booths. "You all know how this works, right? You pick a square of paper out of the hat, and whatever it says on it, that's your booth. No trading with anyone and no complaining if you don't get your first choice."

Everyone nodded. Caroline Pearce, who had a reputation for being a busybody, wriggled up to the front of the line. She wanted to be the first to choose.

Mr. Bowman had written a list of the ten booths up on the blackboard. There was a wide range: a softball throw, a Nerf-ball net, a bottle toss, a shuffleboard game, and darts, among others. The Wheel of Fortune and the water-balloon throw came last on the list.

Caroline picked first and drew the Wheel of Fortune.

Jessica couldn't believe it. "I can't stand it," she moaned to Ellen Riteman and Lila. "Who let *her* go first? She knew how much I wanted it!"

Lila picked the bottle toss, and Ellen got the softball throw. It was Jessica's turn next. She walked up to the front of the room, where Mr.

Bowman was sitting on the edge of his desk. He held out the straw hat and Jessica reached in and took out a little square of paper. The room was quiet as she unfolded it.

At first she couldn't believe her eyes.

"What did you get?" Ellen demanded.

"This isn't fair!" Jessica cried.

Caroline crowded behind to get a look. "She got the water-balloon throw!" she exclaimed.

Jessica looked as if she had just found out the world was coming to an end.

"It won't be that bad, Jessica," Julie Porter said. "Some people have a lot of fun at the water-balloon toss. It's really simple—all you have to do is stand there."

"And maybe everyone will miss," Lila said, trying to make her feel better.

Jessica glared at Caroline. "I should've picked first," she said.

Caroline was so busy gloating about picking the Wheel of Fortune, she didn't even notice how furious Jessica was. Jessica couldn't believe she was stuck with the water-balloon booth. She couldn't imagine anything more horrible. She gathered her books together and stomped out of the room.

"Don't worry," Lila said to Jessica as they walked down the hall. She grinned. "Maybe the

Unicorns can design a waterproof outfit for you so you won't get your clothes all wet."

Jessica narrowed her eyes. "You won't have to," she said. "I'm going to figure out some way to get out of running that dumb booth."

"You can't, Jessica. You heard what Mr. Bowman said. No changing and no backing down."

"I know," Jessica said, frowning. "But I just can't stand there all day letting people throw water balloons at me, Lila!" She looked helplessly at her friend. "There's got to be *some* way out of this."

Two

◇

The next day Jessica was in a terrible mood. Everyone was still talking about how great the fair was going to be and she was getting tired of it. At lunchtime, she heard Lila announce that she was buying a new outfit.

"Just to run the bottle-toss booth?" Ellen asked. "I can't believe it."

Lila ignored Ellen's comment. "What about you, Jess?" she asked. "What are you wearing—plastic wrap?"

Both Ellen and Lila exploded with laughter. Jessica didn't think this was funny at all. "You guys wouldn't be laughing if you were the ones who had to stand there getting balloons full of water thrown at you," she snapped. With that, she jumped up from her seat and stormed out of the cafeteria.

All afternoon everybody teased her about the

water-balloon booth. She couldn't wait until school was over so she could go home and figure out a way to get Caroline to switch with her.

Finally the last bell rang and Jessica was free. She bolted from the classroom and smacked right into Elizabeth in the hall.

"Hi, Lizzie. Are you walking home?" Jessica asked. Maybe Elizabeth would have some ideas.

Elizabeth shook her head. "Olivia and I are working on posters for the fair in the art room." She glanced at her watch. "I won't be home until around five. If someone named Mrs. Sampson calls, will you tell her I'll call her tonight?" She was about to add something but Olivia called her, and she had to hurry off.

Twenty minutes later Jessica unlocked the front door to the Wakefields' attractive, split-level ranch house. "Anyone home?" she called.

Steven, her fourteen-year-old brother, answered with a howl from the kitchen. Jessica groaned. Her day had been bad enough. She wasn't in the mood for Steven's sense of humor that afternoon. "Can't you be human for once in your life?" she said, wandering into the kitchen and opening the refrigerator.

Steven had the newspaper spread out all over the kitchen table. He was reading the want ads and eating ice cream from the carton.

"I guess you couldn't have saved any ice cream

for me," Jessica complained mournfully, sitting down at the table and trying to rearrange the paper so she could read it. Steven ate more than anyone she knew.

"I thought you were trying to watch your weight," Steven said, grinning. Jessica ignored him. She and Elizabeth were both perfectly slim and Steven knew it. He was being a pain, as always.

"Are you looking for a job?" she asked, trying to take her mind off her own problem.

Steven nodded. "I want to get some new speakers for my stereo. Do you think I'd be any good as a waiter?"

Jessica cracked up. "Fat chance. You'd eat all the food before it got to the table."

Steven pretended to take a swipe at her but Jessica leapt out of his way too quickly. Luckily the phone rang and she had an excuse to run out of the room and answer it.

"Hello, is Elizabeth there?" a woman's voice asked politely.

Jessica made a face at Steven from the safety of the living room. "I'm sorry, she's working on a project at school this afternoon," she said. "Can I take a message for her?"

The woman sighed. "Oh, dear. I won't be able to call her back this evening." She paused for a minute. "I'll tell you what. If you wouldn't mind, I could tell you a little bit of what I was going to tell her, and you could pass the message along. Would that be all right?"

"Sure," Jessica said, rummaging for a piece of paper and a pencil.

"My name is Mrs. Sampson," the woman continued. "I was given Elizabeth's name by Amy Sutton. Amy told me Elizabeth was interested in baby-sitting for me this Saturday. Now, I'm not sure how much Amy has told Elizabeth about the job, but Saturday shouldn't be too bad, because two of my children are going to be gone for the day."

Jessica wrote down the number two, frowning. "How many will be left?" she asked.

"Just two." Mrs. Sampson cleared her throat. "It's an all-day job, from ten until five, but it'll just be the two youngest. And they're adorable children," she added.

Jessica wrote down the word "adorable." "Uh-huh," she said.

"Tell her I'll pay her ten dollars an hour, since it is a big day's work," Mrs. Sampson added. "Of course, she'll need to plan some activities for the children. And she'll need to make them lunch. I think that's all she'll need to know."

Jessica looked at the notes she had taken. "Fine. I'll make sure she gets the message," she said.

"If she could just call me back as soon as possible and let me know whether or not she can take the job, I'd be very grateful," Mrs. Sampson said.

Jessica hung up the phone and wrinkled her nose. Poor Elizabeth. Stuck baby-sitting with Mrs. Sampson's kids while everyone else was at the fair. That didn't sound like very much fun.

She was halfway upstairs before it struck her that ten dollars an hour was quite a lot of money for baby-sitting. Ten dollars . . . for seven hours. That meant seventy dollars.

There were a lot of things Jessica could do with seventy dollars. She had a list of things she needed desperately: new perfume, a bathing suit like Lila's, a subscription to *Ingenue* magazine— the list went on and on. She was sure Elizabeth didn't need the money half as much as she did.

Too bad it had to be this Saturday, she thought.

Then it hit her. If she baby-sat for Mrs. Sampson instead of Elizabeth, she'd have a perfect excuse for getting out of the water-balloon booth.

Jessica raced to her bedroom and redialed the number she had written down for Elizabeth. "Mrs. Sampson?"

"Yes?"

"It's Jessica Wakefield, Elizabeth's twin sister. Listen, I just remembered that Elizabeth gave me a message for you," Jessica fibbed.

"Oh, really?"

"She can't baby-sit for you on Saturday because of the sixth-grade fair," Jessica said. She felt a tiny twinge of guilt but justified it by thinking of how grateful Elizabeth would be when she found out she could go to the fair after all. "But as it turns out, *I* could sit for you."

Mrs. Sampson sounded a little confused. "Well, I guess that would be all right. Do you have any experience with small children? My two youngest—Dennis and Susan—are three and five years old."

"Oh, I baby-sit all the time," Jessica said. Actually she had no experience whatsoever with little kids, but how hard could it be? All you did was play with them, or turn on the TV if they got cranky. She couldn't believe her good luck.

"Fine. Why don't you come over at about nine-forty-five Saturday morning?" Mrs. Sampson went on. She gave Jessica her address.

"Great," Jessica said happily, scribbling it down. "I'll see you on Saturday!"

She couldn't believe it. She had found a perfect excuse. Julie couldn't possibly object to an excuse like having to baby-sit.

And on top of it all, she had found herself an incredibly easy way to make a lot of money! She was going to go right out and buy herself something that even Lila didn't own.

*   *   *

Elizabeth got home just after five. "Hi," she said to her older brother, wrinkling her nose at the mess he had made with the newspaper. "Did Mrs. Sampson call?"

Steven grunted, deep in the want ads. "I don't know. Ask Jessica," he said.

Elizabeth ran upstairs to look for her sister. Jessica had a pile of clothing heaped on her bed and was sorting through it with a critical look.

"What do you think, Lizzie? Should I get rid of some of this stuff? I'm planning on buying some new clothes," Jessica told her.

Elizabeth set down her bookbag. "I don't see why," she said. "You already have more clothes than anyone in Sweet Valley." Before Jessica could say anything more she asked, "Did Mrs. Sampson call?"

"Yes, she did," Jessica said matter-of-factly, holding up a navy blue cotton sweater. "Maybe you'd like this," she said generously. "I don't think it's really right for me." She started to hand it to Elizabeth, then changed her mind. "Except if I get a white skirt . . . I love navy and white together . . ."

"Jess," Elizabeth said, "could you just tell me what Mrs. Sampson said about Saturday. I want to call her back before dinner."

"Oh, you don't need to call her back," Jessica said.

"What do you mean? I'm supposed to sit for her on Saturday," Elizabeth exclaimed.

Jessica pretended to examine a speck of something on the sweater. "You can have it," she said at last, handing it back to her sister. "It's really more your style than mine. Plus it has something stuck on it—I think it's glue."

"Thanks a lot," Elizabeth said. She took the sweater, giving it a skeptical look. "Jess, I'm serious about this. Tell me what Mrs. Sampson said. I've had a really long day and I want to straighten this out before I talk to Amy."

"Well," Jessica said, taking a deep breath, "I did you a real favor, Lizzie. You don't have to make a big thing out of it," she added generously. "I knew how badly you wanted to go to the fair on Saturday and how hard it was going to be for you baby-sitting all day when everyone else was at the park having a great time. So I told Mrs. Sampson I'd baby-sit for her kids instead."

Elizabeth stared at her. "You *what*?"

Jessica picked up another sweater. "Don't make a big thing out of thanking me, Lizzie," she said quickly. "I know it was really nice of me and I guess I wouldn't mind if you did me a favor in

return sometime, but really, don't mention it."
She gave Elizabeth a sweet smile.

"Jessica," Elizabeth said, folding her arms
across her chest and giving her sister a stern
look. "Since when do you know the first thing
about taking care of little kids? And anyway,
Amy specifically asked *me* to take the job for
her, not you."

"But I didn't want you to miss the fair!" Jessica cried innocently, her eyes wide.

"Jessica Wakefield, don't lie to me," Elizabeth
said angrily. "If you took that job on Saturday,
you must have a reason." She glared at her sister. "I don't suppose the fact that you got stuck
with the water-balloon booth at the fair has anything to do with it?"

Jessica let out a big sigh. "Boy," she said. "I
don't get it. I try to do one little nice thing for
you, and you act like I'm trying to steal money
from you or something."

"That's another thing," Elizabeth fumed. "I
happen to need the money. I've got a bunch of
birthday presents to buy."

Jessica turned back to the pile of clothes on
her bed. "Well, I really thought I was helping
you out, Lizzie. I'm sorry."

"You know, it's not going to be easy taking
care of those kids," Elizabeth added.

"I know that. And I couldn't stand thinking

of you having to do all that work while the rest of us were having fun at the park!" Jessica cried dramatically.

Elizabeth shook her head. "I hope you know what you're getting into," she said, turning and leaving the room.

Jessica couldn't hide her smile a minute longer. The point wasn't so much what she was getting into as what she was getting out of! Jessica thought that what had happened was nothing short of a miracle. Here she had thought she would be stuck standing around all day getting balloons thrown at her. Instead she'd be far away at the Sampsons' house, sitting around doing nothing, and getting paid for it, too!

Now all she had to do was break the news to Julie Porter—and help her think of someone to take her place at the fair on Saturday.

Three

◆

Lila and Ellen were waiting for Jessica when she got to school on Wednesday morning. "Listen," Lila said with a mischievous smile. "We've been talking about what you should wear on Saturday for the balloon toss. Ellen's got a great idea. We want to make an outfit for you out of plastic garbage bags. That way you won't get your clothes wrecked. Maybe we can even find purple garbage bags." She giggled. Purple was the official color of the Unicorns. "You're going to look so cute, Jess. I'm sure if Bruce Patman comes to the fair he'll think you're the best-looking booth manager!"

Jessica glared at her friends as she opened her locker. Bruce Patman was a seventh grader and, as far as the Unicorns were concerned, one of the cutest guys in the school. "It just so happens I won't be running the water-balloon booth," she retorted. "So you can save your trash bag outfit for someone else."

Ellen and Lila stared at each other. "How'd you manage to squirm your way out of it?" Ellen demanded. "Don't tell me you're going to be a poor sport and quit just because you drew a bad booth."

Jessica flipped her hair back over her shoulder indignantly. "I'm not quitting. It just so happens that I have—" she paused dramatically. "I have a prior commitment, that's all."

Lila snorted. "Prior commitment? Like what?"

Jessica pretended to be busy looking through her locker. "I'm sorry, but I really think I should talk it over with Julie Porter before I tell you any more about it." Taking her books out of her locker, she proceeded to head down the hallway.

Lila and Ellen were right behind her. "I want to see Julie's face when you tell her you won't be showing up at your booth," Lila crowed.

"And I want to hear more about this prior commitment," Ellen added with a giggle.

Jessica shrugged. "Follow me if you like. But you'd better let me be the one to break the news to Julie."

"We will," Lila and Ellen promised in unison.

Julie was looking over some plans for the fair, sitting on one of the benches in the hallway. She was deep in thought.

"Julie, guess what?" Lila cried. "Jessica says she can't do the water-balloon booth!"

"She says she has a prior commitment," Ellen echoed.

"Thanks a lot, you guys," Jessica said. "That's really what I call giving me a chance to break the news."

Julie looked from Ellen to Lila to Jessica with growing horror. "What?" she cried. "Jessica, you're not serious, are you? I've finally got this whole thing figured out—you can't possibly tell me you're backing out now!"

Jessica took a deep breath. This was going to call for some real theatrics. But if anyone could do it, she could, she told herself.

"Listen, I feel incredibly awful about this whole thing," she began. "It's just that when I agreed to be in the fair I had forgotten that I promised to baby-sit on Saturday." She lowered her eyes. "I'm trying not to be a baby, but when you think about it, it's pretty horrible for me. I mean, there you'll be, having the time of your life. And there I'll be . . ."

Lila and Ellen exchanged glances. "I guess it will be pretty hard," Lila said sarcastically. "Since you were so excited about doing the water-balloon booth and everything."

Jessica ignored this. "I'm so sorry, Julie," she repeated. "You know if there were *any* way I could get around it . . ."

Julie shook her head despairingly. "I just wish you had told me about this before. How am I going to find someone to take your place with so little notice?"

Jessica shook her head sadly. "I don't know," she said, shrugging.

"Maybe Jessica has an idea for a replacement," Ellen suggested brightly, ignoring the look Jessica shot her.

"That's right," Lila chirped. "Since she *is* telling you just three days before the fair and all."

Julie looked inquiringly at Jessica. "What do you think, Jess? Any idea of who might be free on Saturday?"

Jessica bit her lip. She shifted her weight from one foot to the other. "Well," she said at last, "I'm not sure whether or not she was really planning on getting involved in anything more than making posters, but I happen to know that Elizabeth is free on Saturday."

"Really?" Julie's face lit up. "Wow, if Elizabeth would step in and take your place . . ."

Jessica swallowed, suddenly feeling nervous.

"You might not want to tell her that I told you she was free," she said quickly. "I mean, knowing her the way I do, I just think you'd have a better chance convincing her if you don't tell her that I gave you her name."

Lila laughed. "Right. And you might have a better chance of making it to the seventh grade in one piece!"

Jessica smiled weakly. She didn't think she wanted to be anywhere near her sister after Julie had finished talking to her!

"Elizabeth!" Julie cried out, hurrying to catch up with her in the lunchroom. "Can I talk to you for a minute?"

Elizabeth and Amy were just sitting down with their trays. "Sure," Elizabeth said. "Have a seat."

Julie sat down beside Elizabeth. "Are you busy on Saturday?"

Elizabeth looked at Amy. She had just finished telling her friend the story of how Jessica had swiped her baby-sitting job. "Actually, I'm not," she said, taking a bite of fruit salad. "Why?"

"Oh, that's great!" Julie sighed with relief. "Listen, I have an *enormous* favor to ask you."

"Sounds urgent," Elizabeth commented.

"It is. I need someone to take over the water-balloon booth on Saturday," Julie explained. "I know it isn't exactly the most popular booth to run, but I think it could be a lot of fun. If I didn't have to supervise the fair I wouldn't mind doing it. But—"

"Wait a minute," Elizabeth said, putting down her spoon. "Isn't that the booth my sister was in charge of?"

"Well . . . yes," Julie said slowly. "But something's come up. Jessica suddenly remembered she had something else she had to do."

Elizabeth stared at Amy, her eyes darkening. "I see," she said shortly. "That's right. She has to baby-sit, isn't that it?"

"Right!" Julie exclaimed with evident relief. "So, would you mind taking her place? I can't tell you what a big favor you'd be doing me—and the whole sixth-grade class."

Elizabeth took a deep breath. "I guess . . . uh . . ." She looked helplessly at Amy. What could she say? It was clear Jessica had maneuvered the whole thing so that she had no choice. "Sure," she said finally.

Amy was staring at her in disbelief. "I can't believe this," she whispered.

"Thanks, Elizabeth. You're the greatest," Julie said, giving her a hug. "Come by Mr. Bowman's room after school today and I'll give you all the info you'll need." She smiled. "But it's pretty simple. Basically all you do is stand there and let people throw water balloons at you!" With that comment she hurried off, leaving Elizabeth and Amy staring after her.

"I can't believe it," Elizabeth said. "I have absolutely never been so furious at her in my whole life."

"It's about time," Amy said. "She's making things worse and worse! First she steals your baby-sitting job, and then she sticks you with the worst possible booth in the entire fair!"

Elizabeth just kept shaking her head. "My very own sister," she cried. "How could she do this to me?" Jessica had gotten her into difficult situations before, but this one had to be the worst.

"I'm going to find her right now!" Elizabeth said furiously. "I'm not kidding, Amy. There's no way that Jessica's going to get away with this!"

"Where is she?" Elizabeth cried, slamming the front door. She hadn't seen Jessica once that afternoon at school. Obviously her sister was trying to avoid her.

Steven was in the kitchen, making his way through the remainder of a cold pizza.

"That's disgusting," Elizabeth said. "Can't you even heat it up first?"

"I like it cold," Steven said. He eyed his little sister with raised eyebrows. "What's your problem? You look like you just met Godzilla or something."

"Where's Jessica?" Elizabeth demanded.

"Out on the patio," Steven answered.

Elizabeth stormed out of the kitchen and found Jessica dozing out in the backyard. Elizabeth stood over her and crossed her arms. Finally Jessica opened one eye.

"What is it?" she said, squinting up at Elizabeth. "Move over, Lizzie. You're blocking the rays."

"You're going to get more than rays!" Elizabeth fumed. "Jessica, would you mind telling me what kind of sneaky behavior made you tell Julie Porter that *I* was free to take over the water-balloon booth on Saturday?"

Jessica rolled over, her expression calm. "Well, you were about the only person I could think of," she said innocently. "What's the big deal, Lizzie? It's not the end of the world." She ignored her sister's angry stare. "Anyway, I couldn't help it. It was unbelievable peer pressure. You should've seen the looks that Ellen and Lila were giving me! I had to come up with *someone!*"

Elizabeth's mouth tightened. "First, you stole my job," she said pointedly. "Then, as if that wasn't bad enough, you gave Julie my name for the worst position in the entire fair! If I'd ever done something like this to you . . ." She let her voice trail off, her eyes flashing with anger.

"Honestly, Elizabeth," Jessica said in her most grown-up voice, "I was trying to do you a favor by letting you take part in the fair in the first place. And it wasn't my fault about the water-balloon booth. Julie asked me if you were busy on Saturday. What could I do—lie?" She widened her eyes. "You're always saying how important it is to be honest."

This made Elizabeth even more furious. "Don't twist things around so it sounds like what you did was right," she cried. "You've been horrible, Jess. And you know it."

Jessica was quiet for a minute. "Don't be mad at me, Lizzie," she pleaded. "Please. I can't stand it when you're so angry."

"Well, you're just going to have to live with it," Elizabeth retorted. "I'd be crazy not to be mad." She paced back and forth in front of her twin.

"By the way, Jess. That baby-sitting job you

stole from me isn't going to be so easy. I've heard the kids are little monsters. And you know what? I hope they are!"

Elizabeth opened the sliding glass doors that led into the dining room. She was about to go into the house, but before she did, she turned around to face her sister and said, "Don't you dare come crying to me for help if things aren't as easy as you expected on Saturday. I'll be busy!"

Four

◇

"I can't believe you're still mad at me," Jessica complained three days later. It was Saturday morning and she was watching Elizabeth get ready for the fair.

"Please," Elizabeth moaned, tying her blond hair back in a ponytail. "Try not to make me want to kill you, Jess." She glanced at her watch. The fair was starting promptly at nine o'clock and she didn't want to be late. She wasn't exactly looking forward to taking Jessica's place at the water-balloon booth, but she knew she would have fun being part of the fair.

As Elizabeth was about to leave, she couldn't resist one last remark. "I hope you don't have too hard a time today, Jess. Amy told me the Sampsons are going to a yacht party out in the harbor. That means you won't be able to call them no matter how awful things get."

Jessica shrugged. "What can be that bad? Don't you know that's why they call it baby-sitting, Lizzie? 'Cause all you do is sit around—and get paid."

Elizabeth grabbed a beach towel from the hall closet. "Something tells me I'm going to need this. Well, Jess, wish me luck. I'm off to get water balloons thrown at me. And I want you to know that every time I get hit I'll be thinking of you—and not with fondness, either."

"Poor Lizzie," Jessica said to herself as she watched her sister disappear downstairs. There was no denying she had maneuvered things to her own advantage but it was too late to change anything now.

An hour later Jessica rang the Sampsons' doorbell. She'd brought a backpack stuffed with the latest issue of *Ingenue* magazine, a couple of paperbacks, and even some homework. Jessica was looking forward to a nice, relaxing day curled up in a chair reading. Maybe she could even coax the kids outside and sit in the sun.

Mrs. Sampson opened the door on the second ring. "Oh, hello, Jessica," she said. Jessica was surprised to see that Mrs. Sampson looked completely worn out. It was only ten o'clock in the morning. "I'm glad you're here," Mrs. Sampson went on. "Ted and I have had a crazy morning.

We're running late so I'll have to give you instructions quickly."

A tiny, angelic-looking boy peered out from behind his mother's skirt, looking up at Jessica with a curious expression on his face. "This is Dennis," Mrs. Sampson said. "Dennis, say hi to Jessica. Jessica's going to be taking care of you today while Mommy and Daddy are out on the big boat I told you about."

Dennis stuffed his finger in his mouth and looked up skeptically at Jessica, who wriggled her fingers at him.

"Hi, Dennis!" she cooed, bending down to pat him on the head. Dennis backed away, blinking at her with wide blue eyes.

"What a sweet boy," Jessica said politely.

"Dennis has been having a little tummy trouble," Mrs. Sampson said. "If he says his stomach hurts, give him . . ." She led Jessica into the kitchen where she rummaged through several cupboards, finally coming up with a bottle of green-colored medicine. "Give him this. He doesn't like it, but it'll help settle his stomach."

"Uh . . . sure," Jessica said weakly.

"Susan! Come meet the baby-sitter," Mrs. Sampson called. When there was no response she called again, and after a long pause a little girl with red curls wandered into the kitchen, scratching a tiny red spot on her arm.

"Mommy," she said softly, "something bit me on the arm." She looked shyly at Jessica. "You said Amy was coming," she said accusingly.

Mrs. Sampson gave a small, embarrassed laugh. "She's just a little bashful with strangers, Jessica. Now, Ted and I are going to be at a party on a friend's yacht. I think the easiest thing to do if you have an emergency is to call Karen Henry, my next-door neighbor. I've stuck her number on the refrigerator."

"Fine," Jessica said. She was ready for Mr. and Mrs. Sampson to leave so she could settle down with her magazine. She hoped there was plenty of good food around the house. This job was going to be easy.

"I left lunch for Dennis and Susan and you in the refrigerator. Do you have a microwave at home?" When Jessica nodded, Mrs. Sampson said, "Great. Just reheat the spaghetti for them. Dennis won't eat it unless it's hot." She looked around anxiously. "I can't think of anything else . . ."

"Do either of them need a nap?" Jessica asked hopefully.

"I don't think there's much chance of that," Mrs. Sampson said, shaking her head. "They're both pretty energetic." She tousled Susan's hair. "But you shouldn't have too much on your hands. The other children are gone for the whole day. Gretchen's hiking with her Brownie troop and Peter's spending the day at a friend's house."

"Mommy," Susan said, tugging on her mother's skirt. "Why can't me and Dennis come with you?"

Mrs. Sampson let out a small sigh. "She's at that stage," she told Jessica as if she were revealing a secret. Jessica wasn't at all sure what "that stage" meant.

Mrs. Sampson leaned over to give her daughter a kiss. "Remember what you promised Mommy—that you'd be extra good today for Jessica?"

Susan looked at her doubtfully.

"Oh, before I forget," Mrs. Sampson said, turning back to Jessica. "Let me show you something." She led Jessica through the warm, comfortable family room to a set of French doors. "This," she said dramatically, throwing open the doors, "is the living room."

Jessica peered through the doors. The room was decorated in white and light gray, not very practical for a family with four little kids. Otherwise there was nothing exceptional about it.

"You're probably wondering how this room has stayed in one piece," Mrs. Sampson said, before Jessica could say a word. "Well, we have one rule in the Sampson household. And it's a golden rule, not to be broken under any circumstances. No one goes into the living room." She took a large key out of a box on the mantel and ceremoniously locked the French doors, putting the key up on the fourth shelf of the bookcase in the family room. "The kids know better than to go in there, but just to be on the safe side, I'm going to lock it. OK?"

"Sure," Jessica said. She couldn't understand why Mrs. Sampson was bothering. Dennis looked like such a little angel, sitting on the couch with his short, chubby legs thrust out in front of him. And Susan was a beautiful little girl. Jessica was almost tempted to play dolls with her for part of the morning. If the issue of *Ingenue* didn't look so enticing, she would have suggested it.

After what seemed like an eternity, Mr. Sampson came downstairs, tying his tie. Dennis and Susan were quiet and sweet-tempered when they were saying goodbye to their parents and Jessica felt a little rush of affection for them. This was the life, she thought. She had finally found a job that suited her perfectly. All she had to do was smile at the kids every once in a while and reheat spaghetti. For seventy dollars, that wasn't bad!

"Well," she said cheerfully, hearing the Sampsons' car pull out of the driveway. "I guess it's just the three of us now, huh?"

Dennis still had his finger stuck in his mouth and Susan was rubbing furiously at the pink spot on her arm, which was starting to get swollen. Jessica cleared her throat. "Maybe you should think of something to do," she said, looking longingly at her backpack.

"My beesting hurts," Susan complained, rubbing harder and harder at her arm.

Jessica walked over to her to have a look. "It isn't a beesting, it's a mosquito bite," she said. "If you just leave it alone, it will stop hurting. You're about to rub your whole arm off."

Susan stared at her, her eyes widening in horror. But before Jessica could say another word the phone rang.

"Phone! Phone!" Dennis cried.

"I'll get it," Susan cried, racing for the phone.

Jessica snatched the receiver away from her. "*I'll* get it," she corrected the child, whose pout deepened to a scowl. She could hear a faint buzz in the receiver.

"Jessica?" a familiar voice inquired. It was Lila Fowler.

"Lila, where are you? Why aren't you at the fair?" Jessica demanded, watching Susan and Dennis wander off to the back of the family room, where the games were kept.

"I am," Lila said. Jessica heard more buzzing and some static. "I'm calling from my brand-new cordless phone. I brought it with me so we could all make calls today if we have to. Julie's got the base plugged in over in the guardhouse but I'm keeping it right here by my side." She giggled. "I thought you might like an update on the fair from time to time."

"What a great idea!" Jessica exclaimed. She was watching out of the corner of her eye as Susan reached up to take a box from one of the shelves and a pile of games came crashing down.

"What was that?" Lila demanded. "Are you in trouble over there already? Maybe I'd better give you my phone number so you can call if disaster strikes." She giggled.

"Ha-ha," Jessica said flatly. She turned her back so she didn't have to look at the mess Susan and Dennis were making. "This is the cushiest job in the whole world," she said under her breath. "Seventy bucks for doing nothing! Two of the kids aren't even here."

"That's lucky," Lila said. "As far as I'm concerned, even one kid is too many." Something buzzed loudly and Lila added, "Your sister's the star of the fair, Jess. She's gotten more money so far than any other booth. And she hasn't even been hit yet!"

Jessica felt a sudden pang. For the first time that morning she wished she was at the fair. "Well, it's really fun here," she said as brightly as she could. "I mean, incredibly fun. Make sure to tell Elizabeth how much fun I'm having."

"OK," Lila said. "So, let me give you this number in case you need to call."

Jessica obligingly wrote down the number. "But it's not likely I'll *need* to call," she said. "I'm telling you, Li, this job's a cinch."

"Well, good. I'd better go," Lila added. "I've got someone who wants to do the bottle toss— believe it or not." And the next thing Jessica knew the static had disappeared and Lila was gone.

Jessica set the phone down, feeling another pang. Maybe she should have let Elizabeth baby-sit after all. It had never occurred to Jessica that you could duck and avoid getting hit. She wouldn't even have had to get that wet.

Susan was kicking at checker pieces with her small foot. "I'm bored," she cried. "I'm bored, bored, bored, bored, bored."

Dennis apparently liked the sound of this because he started echoing his sister. "Me, too," he said. "Bored!"

Jessica marched across the room and opened her backpack, taking out her magazine. "I'll tell you what," she said. "How about if you two find something to read, and we all play library?"

Dead silence followed this suggestion. Jessica sat down and opened the magazine and Susan started to cry. "My beesting is bleeding," she hollered.

Jessica sighed heavily and set the magazine down. "Let me see," she said, coming over to take a look. Sure enough, a minuscule drop of blood was coming from the spot Susan had been scratching.

"I don't think it's too serious," Jessica said.

Susan gave her a sullen look. "It hurts," she muttered.

Dennis kicked at the checker pieces. "Why don't you think up a game for us to play? Our other baby-sitter always thinks up games," he said.

Jessica looked at him. "Why don't you tell me what sort of games you like?" she suggested diplomatically.

Susan began to cry again. "It hurts. It hurts and you don't even care!"

"Listen, I've got an idea," Jessica said, trying not to sound irritated. "Let's all just sit down now and think about what we're going to do this morning, all right? We have lots and lots of choices."

Dennis picked up the cardboard box with the rest of the checker pieces in it and turned it upside down.

"Dennis!" Jessica scolded. Then she stopped herself. "That wasn't a very good idea," she said, trying not to sound angry. "Why don't we all sit down and try to figure out what the most fun thing to do next could be." She cast a last look at her magazine, which was lying face down on the couch. Well, as soon as she came up with something for them to do and got their interest, she'd have the rest of the day all to herself. They were bound to be a little bit cranky right after their parents left, but in a minute or two they'd settle down. She was sure of it.

"Those are *my* checkers," Susan whined, tugging at the box.

Dennis started to cry and Jessica decided it was time to take serious action. "OK, you guys, listen up," she said. Both children turned to her, but neither looked particularly attentive. "*I*," Jessica announced, "just got an absolutely fabulous idea."

Neither of them said anything. They just stood there staring at her. And Jessica had no idea what to say next.

The truth was, she didn't have the faintest idea how to entertain them!

Five

◇

Caroline Pearce was having the time of her life. The Wheel of Fortune was the best booth at the whole fair.

"Step right up!" she hollered. "Come right up here and spin the wheel!"

Caroline had made the wheel herself, with Julie Porter's help. It was almost as big as she was, and colorfully painted. Each contestant got one spin and a chance to find out his or her fortune, which Caroline read in her best dramatic voice. She had already told Bruce Patman that he would be the richest man in the world and Ken Matthews that he was going to have ten children.

Lila called over to her from her own booth. "Hey, want to trade? Wouldn't you rather do the bottle toss for a while and let me do the Wheel of Fortune?"

Caroline chewed a strand of carrot-red hair. "Nah," she said.

Lila shrugged. "Fine with me. The bottle toss is the best booth anyway," she said in her most stuck-up voice.

Julie Porter came over to see how everything was going. "I can't believe how great the fair is going!" she cried, looking back and forth at Lila and Caroline whose booths were facing each other at one end of the park. "Now, don't forget to take a break soon and get yourselves some food or something. I want you to have fun, too—not just work."

That was all Lila needed to hear. She was off like a shot to try out the water-balloon booth. She wanted to see how Elizabeth was holding up.

To her surprise, Elizabeth seemed to be having a blast. She and Amy were dissolved in giggles when Lila came over. Winston Egbert had just brought over a delivery from the concession stand and they were busy trying to divide a doughnut into equal halves. Elizabeth wasn't even wet.

"How's the water-balloon business? Having fun?" Lila asked in a teasing voice.

Elizabeth gave her a big smile. "As a matter of fact, I am," she said. She and Amy winked at each other. "What do you think Jessica's doing right now?" Elizabeth asked her friend.

Amy shuddered. "I hate to think about it," she said, taking a bite of doughnut. "There's no telling what those kids might be up to."

Jessica looked from Dennis to Susan, racking her brains for something wonderful to do. What were you supposed to do with a three- and a five-year-old?

"Let's make card houses," she said brightly, seeing a pack of cards that had fallen off one of the shelves.

"I hate cards," Susan said miserably.

Dennis stuck out his lower lip. "I want to make a card house," he said. He turned imploringly to Jessica. "Let's make card houses," he begged.

Susan stamped her feet, her red curls shaking furiously. "I hate making card houses," she yelled.

Jessica put her hands over her ears. "You don't have to yell," she said as calmly as she could. "What *would* you like to do?"

Susan poked at the swollen red spot on her arm. "I know," she said brightly after a long pause. "Let's take out all of Mommy's jewelry and pretend that we're Queen of England."

Jessica looked despairingly at her. "I don't think that your mommy would like that very much. Let's try to think of something else."

"I hate jewelry," Dennis said, his eyes filling with tears.

"Maybe we could all go outside," Jessica suggested, giving her magazine one last sad look.

But now that Dennis and Susan had discovered how much fun it was to disagree with each other, there was no chance of getting them to want to do the same thing. Dennis wanted to go outside and Susan didn't. "I'm scared of that bee," she said.

"Susan," Jessica cried. "That's a mosquito bite, not a beesting."

"I don't like you," Susan said, sniffling and wiping her nose on her arm. "I want Mommy to come back from the boat."

"Susan," Jessica began, deciding a different approach was going to be necessary, "will you be a really helpful girl and help me think of something that all three of us can play together?"

Dennis was getting fingerprints all over the glass doors that led to the living room. "Let's play in there," he suggested brightly.

"No," Jessica said. "No one goes in the living room. You know that. Let's see. We could watch TV," she said, sorry to have to use the last resort so quickly.

By some miracle, both Dennis and Susan brightened at this suggestion. But Jessica wasn't out of trouble yet. The minute the set was warmed up, the two of them started fighting over the remote control.

"Gimme that!" Dennis cried, yanking it out of Susan's hands. "I wanna watch cartoons!"

Susan kicked his leg as hard as she could. "I want to watch the Flory Daniel show," she hollered, snatching back the control.

Jessica plucked it out of her hands and scowled down at both of them. "I'm going to count to three," she said. "And if you two haven't found a show you both want to watch, I'm turning off the set."

That didn't turn out to be such a good idea, either. By the count of three Dennis was crying and Susan had a big scratch on her arm, right above her inflamed mosquito bite. Jessica didn't feel very triumphant turning off the TV set. She stared helplessly at her rebellious little charges, wondering what on earth to do next.

"My stomach hurts," Dennis complained. "I need some medicine."

Jessica couldn't believe anyone would voluntarily submit to swallowing that foul-looking medicine in the kitchen, but she didn't want him to get sick to his stomach. "OK, come with me," she said, leading him into the kitchen and leaving Susan sitting innocently on the couch. Maybe this was what they needed, she thought, grateful for the silence once the two children were separated.

"Here, sit up on this stool for a minute," Jessica instructed. She had to hoist Dennis up and she couldn't believe how heavy he was.

"I want some ice cream," Dennis said, wrinkling his nose when she offered him a spoonful of the green medicine.

Jessica couldn't hide her annoyance much longer. "Look, you said your stomach hurt. Do you want your medicine or don't you?"

Dennis squeezed his eyes shut and opened his mouth a centimeter—just wide enough for Jessica to poke in the tip of the spoon.

"Ugh!" he squealed, spitting the medicine right back at her.

Jessica flung the spoon into the sink, screaming. Little green drops were splattered all over her shirt. "Dennis Sampson, you are in *trouble!*" she yelled.

Dennis's eyes filled with tears. "It tasted so bad," he said, defending himself. "Don't yell at me."

Jessica was scrubbing furiously at her shirt with a paper towel. She couldn't believe what monsters these two kids were. What in the world was she going to do, trapped here with them all day?

Suddenly she heard something that made her cock her head. "What's that?" she asked Dennis, turning around. It was coming from the family room. It sounded like paper being torn up.

"Susan," Jessica called, trying not to sound alarmed. "What are you doing in there?"

Susan was humming cheerfully. "I'm making a collage, like we do in kindergarten," she called back.

Jessica helped Dennis off the stool. "Let's go see what your sister is making," she said. "It sounds like fun, doesn't it?"

Dennis didn't answer, but he trudged behind her into the family room. Susan was sitting in the middle of the carpet, surrounded by torn up bits of glossy paper and busily tearing more— out of Jessica's magazine, which was almost completely destroyed. Jessica's mouth dropped open. For a split second she wanted to laugh. This couldn't be happening, she thought. It just couldn't.

Elizabeth warned her the kids could be trouble. But who would have thought things could get this bad?

Elizabeth had just gotten back from a short break and was taking up her position behind the table at the water-balloon booth. Her short tour around the park had proven to her that the fair was a huge success. Lila's bottle toss was pretty popular, and so was Caroline Pearce's

Wheel of Fortune. But Elizabeth had to admit that her own booth had seen more traffic than most. And so far no one had managed to hit her. She was actually having fun, and she felt a little bad now about reacting so strongly when Jessica had volunteered her name for the job. It wasn't that bad after all!

Bruce Patman strolled over. "Hi, Elizabeth," he drawled. "I've been saving the best for last. Can I have a try?"

Elizabeth had never liked Bruce. She knew some of the girls in the sixth grade thought he was cute, including her sister. But she thought he was a spoiled show-off. "Go ahead," she said. "You know the rules. It costs fifty cents and you only get one try. You have to stand behind the line," she added.

Bruce scooped a red balloon out of the garbage can next to the table. It wriggled around in his hands, and he laughed. "This thing is slippery!"

"If you hit me, you win a ticket," Elizabeth added. All booths worked by the same principle—winners got a ticket, and at the end of the day the tickets could be traded in for prizes.

"Better get ready," Bruce said. A small crowd had gathered to watch.

"Duck, Liz!" Ken Matthews yelled.

Elizabeth turned to look at him, and when

she did, she lost the split second she needed to slip out of the way of Bruce's shot. The water balloon hit her right in the chest, and water went spraying in every direction.

A few of Bruce's seventh-grade friends cheered and Elizabeth stared at them, wiping water off her face and trying to wring out her hair. She was about to get mad and then all of a sudden she realized it didn't feel so bad. In this hot weather, the water balloon actually felt kind of good!

Elizabeth was still wiping herself off when Lila came hurrying over with her cordless phone.

"It's for you, Elizabeth. It's your sister," Lila said, handing her the phone.

Elizabeth grabbed it. "I'm glad you called," she said wryly. "I was just thinking I really owe you a favor, Jess."

Jessica didn't seem to notice her sarcasm. "I'm glad you feel that way," she gasped. "Because I really need help. These kids are absolute, total monsters! If I'd had any idea I never, ever would've taken this job." Her voice had a funny echo to it. "I'm actually in the Sampsons' hall closet. This was the only place I could find to call you from where the kids couldn't hear."

Elizabeth finished wiping the water from one arm. "This isn't exactly a great moment to ask me for help," she said. "I just got hit by a water balloon. Besides, I told you when you stole my job not to come crying to me for help."

Something crashed next to the phone. "Whoops, I think I just knocked over the umbrella rack," Jessica said. "Lizzie, look. I'm so sorry I stuck you with that booth. But you've got to forgive me and try to help me think of something to do with these kids! I'm afraid they're going to kill each other."

A group of fifth graders approached the booth. "Can I buy a water balloon?" one of them asked.

Elizabeth sighed. "Look, Jess, I have to go. You're just going to have to do the best you can," she said. "After all, you're the one who wanted to baby-sit so badly." And before Jessica could say another word she put the phone down on the table, cutting off the connection.

"Time to try something new," Jessica mumbled to herself, clambering out of the closet with the phone. If Elizabeth wasn't going to help her, she'd just have to come up with a scheme of her own.

But she didn't have time to think. She hadn't even made it back to the family room when she heard a terrible crash, followed by two short screams.

"Help!" Dennis hollered. "Susan's trying to hurt me!"

Jessica dropped the phone and raced into the kitchen, where she found Susan kneeling on top of her little brother, a spoon raised ominously over him in her tiny fist. Next to the two children a box of ice cream, almost empty, was melting on the floor.

"He was trying to eat all the ice cream," Susan explained tearfully when Jessica had pried her off the little boy.

Dennis's face was streaked with ice cream and dried tears. Jessica looked at him in horror. "Don't tell me," she said. "Did you really eat all that ice cream by yourself?"

Dennis stared at her, his hands on his stomach. "My tummy hurts," he said. His eyes had a glassy sheen to them, and Jessica grabbed the counter to steady herself.

The situation couldn't possibly get any worse, could it?

Six

◇

"OK," Jessica said, in her most authoritative voice. "We're all going into the family room and we're going to play a game. All three of us, together. Does everyone understand?"

Susan stomped into the family room. "I want to play in the living room," she cried. "Mommy always lets us play in the living room when we have baby-sitters."

"She does not," Jessica called back, leaning down to give Dennis a hand. He was still holding his stomach and didn't look like he felt very well. "Come on, Dennis. Let's go play a really fun game. That'll take your mind off your stomach."

Dennis didn't look convinced but he followed her into the family room, where Susan was busily lifting every single object she could find, hunting for something.

"Mommy hid the key to the living room but I bet I can find it," Susan sang out, ignoring Jessica's warning looks.

"Susan," Jessica fumed, "either you come over here and play a game with your little brother and me, or—" She broke off as Susan met her angry gaze with a cool stare. Or what? She hadn't asked Mrs. Sampson how to discipline the kids. She had just assumed that there wasn't any reason. They had been so well-behaved when their parents were around.

Dennis was starting to groan, clutching his stomach. "Jessica," he gulped, "I think—I think—"

"Uh-oh," Susan gasped, alarmed. "That's the way Dennis always looks right before—"

"Come with me quickly," Jessica yelled, scooping the little boy up in her arms and racing him into the bathroom. They made it just in time. Dennis threw up into the toilet while Jessica held his head, trying to comfort him.

Within minutes she was sponging off his face and trying to calm him down.

"I guess I ate too much ice cream," Dennis said sheepishly.

Jessica shook her head slowly from side to side. Why was this happening to her? Why was everything going from bad to worse?

Dennis wiped his eyes and scrambled to his feet with renewed energy. Now that he'd gotten sick he felt better again and was raring to go. And Jessica couldn't stop him from racing off to join his sister because the telephone rang.

A high-pitched voice asked for Susan.

"Who is this?" Jessica asked suspiciously.

"It's me, Gretchen," the little girl's voice squeaked out. "Are you the baby-sitter?"

"Yes," Jessica said mournfully. "What is it, Gretchen? I thought you were off hiking with the Girl Scouts."

"Brownies," Gretchen corrected her. "And I was. I mean, I am. But the scoutleader just fell down and sprained her ankle and we're waiting for a doctor. The two other group leaders think they may have to drive us all home and I was wondering—"

Jessica heard a crash coming from the family room. "Gretchen, I have to go," she exclaimed, setting the phone down. She snatched it up a second later. "Don't hang up, I'll be right back." She tore into the family room to see what was going on.

To her horror, she saw Dennis had kicked over a copper vase full of dried flowers and scattered them all over the floor. He was trying his hardest to wriggle after Susan in her mad treasure hunt for the key to the living room. "Stop it, you two!" Jessica screamed, putting her hands menacingly on her hips. "I mean it!"

She raced back to the telephone and picked it up. "Gretchen?"

But only a dial tone answered her. Gretchen had hung up.

"Great," Jessica muttered. "That's just great. All I need is for her to come home right now!"

Susan was busily climbing up the bookshelves, taking each book off and handing it down to her brother, when Jessica came back into the family room. "This time I really mean it," Jessica seethed, putting her arms around Susan from behind and stepping backwards with the wriggling child in her grip. "I've had it, Susan. Either you sit down and play some sort of nice, civilized game with your brother and me or you go straight to your room and stay there!"

Susan wriggled wildly. "Put—me—down!" she cried. And with one mighty twist she managed to leap free, knocking into the bookshelf and sending the living room key flying in a long arc till it landed on the carpet at Dennis's feet.

"The key!" Susan and Dennis both yelled at once.

Jessica dove for it, but it was too late. The children were too quick for her. Dennis grabbed it first, then Susan wrestled it out of his hand.

"Give me that," Jessica ordered, stretching out her hand.

Dennis and Susan stared at her, wide-eyed.

Susan was just opening her mouth to say something when the doorbell rang.

"Oh, no," Jessica groaned. "What else could possibly happen?" She gave Susan the sternest look she could muster. "If either one of you so much as goes near that living room door you're going to be in the very worst trouble there is. Get it?" She raced off to open the front door, trying to look back to make sure neither of them had budged.

Mrs. Sampson had double-locked the front door and it took her almost a minute to unlock it, undo the chain, and yank it open. A boy, who must have been about eight, was standing there, his face all puckered up as if he were about to cry. One look at the way he was scratching his arm and Jessica knew he must be a Sampson kid.

"What do you want?" she said warily.

The boy edged toward her. "I'm Peter Sampson," he said. "I was at my friend Joey's house but we got in a really bad fight and I accidentally hit him and . . ." He looked longingly past her into the front hall. "So I came back," he said hopefully. "Joey wasn't any fun anyway. It's much more fun at home."

Jessica stared at him. What was she supposed to do now? She couldn't tell him to go away. It was his house, not hers. But she wasn't getting paid to sit for three kids. Susan and Dennis were already much more than she could handle. There was no way she could take care of one more and keep them all entertained and happy.

"I think you should just go back, Peter," Jessica said firmly, trying to sound cheerful and kind without wavering. "Your mother expected you to spend the whole day at Joey's house and I'm sure Joey's mother did, too. In fact, I'll bet she's really upset. She's probably wondering where you are right now."

"Uh-unh," Peter said, still scratching his arm. "She said she'd prefer it if I didn't come back today, 'cause of Joey and me getting in such a bad fight."

Jessica took a deep breath. It looked as if she had no choice. "Well, I guess you'll just have to stay here, then," she said sadly. She opened the door wider and Peter raced back to the family room to look for Susan and Dennis.

"I've got to call Elizabeth," Jessica said aloud, peeking in to see how bad things had gotten. She was beginning to realize she had a disaster on her hands. And when she saw the doors to the living room wide open she knew she couldn't wait another second. She had to get help and fast!

"Poor thing," Amy said, helping Elizabeth wipe herself off after her latest dousing. The water-balloon booth was getting more and more popular as Elizabeth's record got worse. The last four people who had taken a turn had all managed to hit her. After remaining dry for most of the morning, now she was sopping wet.

"I'm going to have to come up with a special way to pay Jessica back for this," Elizabeth said.

"Hey, Elizabeth. It looks like Lila wants you again."

"I can't imagine what she wants," Elizabeth said sarcastically, as Lila ran toward her waving the cordless phone.

"Guess who?" Lila said, handing it to Elizabeth.

Elizabeth was in no mood to talk to her twin. "What is it, Jess?" she said grouchily into the phone.

Jessica sounded really upset. "You won't believe it," she gasped. "Just when things were really getting bad, one of the other kids showed up! I wasn't doing so well when it was just two of them. What am I going to do now that they're multiplying?"

Elizabeth was still drying herself off. "Look," she said, "I'm drenched from water balloons, and you're calling to tell me you can't handle a simple baby-sitting job that you stole from me!"

"It isn't one bit simple!" Jessica cried. "You wouldn't think so if you saw these kids. They're monsters. You have to help me, Lizzie. Otherwise the house will be torn to bits."

"You should've thought of that before you stole the job," Elizabeth said. She shook the last few drops of water out of her hair. "Sorry, Jess, but you're on your own this time. I have to get back in the booth before someone starts throwing wet balloons at Amy."

"But, Liz—" Jessica started to wail.

Elizabeth hung up. She felt a tiny twinge of remorse, imagining how unhappy Jessica must be. But she reminded herself that Jessica had brought all the problems on herself.

Anyway, how bad could it be? It was only a simple daytime baby-sitting job. She was sure her sister was exaggerating about how bad it was.

Jessica's hands flew up to cover her eyes in horror. "What—what—" she stammered. She couldn't believe what she saw.

All three children were in the living room— the only room in the house that was off-limits. Dennis was jumping up and down on the white couch with his tennis shoes on. Susan was playing some kind of make-believe game with the collection of Wedgwood china. And Peter was putting a tape into his father's very expensive tape deck.

"Peter, please don't touch that," Jessica begged, rushing forward and snatching the tape out of his hands.

But it was clear that Susan and Dennis had already told their older brother not to listen to Jessica. He just rolled his eyes at her. "I want to hear this tape," he whined.

Jessica didn't know what to do first. Nothing she did seemed to work, anyway. When she stamped her foot and ordered them out of the living room, they ignored her. She was sure any minute now they were going to destroy the entire room.

As soon as Peter was done turning on the music he looked around for something else to do. When his eye fell on his younger brother, he said, "Know what Joey and me were going to do just before I left his house?"

"What?" Susan asked, twisting a red curl around her finger and looking at her older brother adoringly. Jessica had a feeling Peter wasn't a very good influence on Susan.

"We were going to give each other tattoos. Like on TV," Peter said.

"Wow!" Susan's eyes shone.

"Wanna help me give Dennis some tattoos?" Peter continued.

"Yeah!" Susan cried.

"No way," Jessica cried.

But it was impossible to stop them. Susan rushed out of the room and quickly returned with her tattoo set. Peter held Dennis down while she proceeded to decorate every bit of his arms and legs that she could reach.

"Let me go! Let me go!" Dennis kept crying. Susan and Peter both called him a crybaby and continued to cover him with tattoos. Jessica would have admired their persistence if she wasn't ready to strangle them instead.

She was doing her very best to pull Susan and Peter off Dennis when she heard what sounded like pounding on the back door. "Oh, no!" she moaned. "Now what?"

Susan jumped up and raced to the back to see who it was while Jessica tried to wipe some of the paint off Dennis.

"It's Gretchen! She's home!" she heard Susan cry.

"Gretchen?" Jessica repeated blankly, staring at Peter.

Then, with a sinking feeling in her stomach, she remembered. Gretchen must have been sent home from her hike.

Jessica didn't know whether to laugh or cry.

Seven

"Hi," Gretchen said, poking her head into the living room. "Wow," she added. "We've never had a baby-sitter who let us play in the *living room* before!" She ran over to join Dennis and Peter on the couch and looked appreciatively at her little brother's tattoos. "Neat," she said. "I want some, too!"

Gretchen was a plump, cheerful-looking seven-year-old, old enough to be reasoned with, Jessica thought. "Look, Gretchen, I don't know what happened to your hiking trip, but I need some help," she said. "Your brothers and sister—"

Gretchen just stared at her and Jessica had the uncomfortable feeling that asking for help may not have been the best tactic after all. She was going to have to act more authoritative, fast.

"I want you to help me get everyone outside so we can play under the sprinkler," Jessica said with sudden inspiration. That way she could get the tattoos rinsed off Dennis and get rid of the kids' excess energy before lunch. "And another thing. There're too many of you around for me to keep an eye on. Peter, you're just going to have to go back to Joey's house for the rest of the afternoon." She marched over to the phone. "Tell me Joey's phone number. I'll call and say you'll be right over."

Peter looked sheepishly at Jessica. "Maybe you shouldn't call him," he said slowly.

Jessica glared at him. "Why not? Your mother said you were supposed to spend the whole day there, and that's what you're going to do. Four of you is too many. It just isn't fair."

Gretchen was busy applying a tattoo to Susan's arm. "Joey's last name is Sorrenson." She told Jessica his phone number. "But when he and Peter have been fighting . . ."

Jessica dialed the number without waiting for Gretchen to finish. A little boy answered the phone. "Is this Joey?" Jessica asked. When the boy said yes, she continued, "I'm Peter's babysitter. I was wondering—"

"No way," Joey said. "Tell Peter I never want to talk to him again. He broke one of my best robots," he added. "And he scratched me on the arm. I never want to see him again as long as I live!"

"I guess that means he wouldn't be welcome to come back for the rest of the day," Jessica said weakly. Gretchen and Peter gave each other triumphant smiles.

Joey made a rude noise. "I hate his guts. Tell him that," he said. And before Jessica could say another word, Joey Sorrenson had hung up on her.

"Stop giving each other those looks," she said angrily to Gretchen and Peter after she hung up the phone. "Come on, put on your bathing suits. We're all going outside—" She grabbed Susan by one hand and Dennis by the other—"to play under the sprinkler." She glared at Gretchen and Peter. "All five of us. *Right now.*"

"I hate the sprinkler," Susan moaned. But by now Jessica was so angry she didn't care.

Once everyone had changed, she dragged the two littlest Sampsons outside and Gretchen and Peter trudged behind, curious to see what she'd do.

For the next half hour Jessica had to congratulate herself on her brilliant idea. Gretchen and Peter decided jumping around in the sprinkler was cool, which meant that Dennis and Susan liked it, too. And Jessica managed to scrub most of the tattoos off the two little kids. Dennis still had a bit of color on his arms and legs, but he was a lot cleaner than he had been when they started. She might have been able to enjoy her victory even longer if Peter hadn't suddenly announced that he was hungry.

"We haven't had our lunch," Dennis said accusingly. He had forgotten all about the ice cream by now. Apparently his stomach felt better. "I'm hungry," he added, outraged, as if Jessica had been intentionally starving them all.

"We can eat in a little while," Jessica said vaguely, dreading the thought of four kids loose in the kitchen. But there was no putting it off once the idea had been brought up.

"I'm starved. Starved, starved, starved," Susan chanted.

"Me, too," Gretchen said. "Our dumb troop leader sprained her ankle before we even got to eat any lunch."

"I'm the hungriest," Peter said sulkily. "I'm the one who's growing the most."

While the kids argued about who was the hungriest, Jessica sneaked off to the kitchen to investigate the contents of the refrigerator. She found the pot of spaghetti Mrs. Sampson had told her about. But when she unwrapped it, her worst fears were confirmed. There was enough for three at the most. Certainly not five. Even if Jessica didn't eat anything, there still wouldn't be enough for all four kids.

"I want ice cream," Dennis cried, swooping into the kitchen.

"I want peanut-butter-and-bacon on rye bread toast," Peter sang out.

"I want frozen yogurt with hot blueberries and bananas," Gretchen said. "Then I want—"

"We're having spaghetti," Jessica said loudly. "That's what your mother left and that's what you're having. I don't want to hear any complaints. Got it?"

Susan started to cry. "She's mean," she said, sinking into a chair and burying her face in her hands.

Jessica looked at the microwave and frowned. She couldn't remember now what Mrs. Sampson had said about it. *Does she set it on high or low?*

High, she decided. *And it probably needs a long time to get really hot.* She didn't want any of these bratty kids complaining, especially since there was barely enough for each of them to get a taste. She set the microwave on high for eight minutes, and while the spaghetti was reheating, tried to get everyone something to drink. Susan wanted milk, Dennis wanted cola with ice cream in it, Peter wanted just plain cola, Gretchen wanted chocolate milk, and then of course Susan wanted chocolate milk, too, and Dennis wanted plain cola, no ice cream. Jessica was trying very hard not to scream by the time the bell rang on the microwave.

She took the bowl out and stared at it suspiciously. "Is it supposed to sizzle this way?" she asked.

"Ugh," Peter said, getting up from the table to take a look. "It looks like rubbery strings."

"Maybe you put it in for too long," Susan said. "Daddy always complains things taste like rubber if they're in too long."

Jessica took an experimental bite. The spaghetti tasted awful. Worse, it was turning from a sizzling mess to a solid rock.

"It's a spaghetti brick," Peter said.

"I'm hungry," Susan moaned.

"Me, too," Dennis said.

Jessica looked at them in despair. Now what? She couldn't expect them to eat this now. She had to admit it looked disgusting. But what else was there?

"I thought the soup at the Sorrensons' house looked gross. But this is *really* gross," Peter said mournfully.

"All right, all right. What else is there to eat?" Jessica asked.

"Let's make microwave popcorn!" Dennis hollered. Then everyone had a suggestion. Fried chicken. Cookies. Graham cracker, melted chocolate, and toasted marshmallow sandwiches. Jessica ignored all of their suggestions as she rummaged wildly through the refrigerator. To her immense relief, she found a package of bologna. She put a loaf of bread on the table and a jar of peanut butter, and the bologna and mustard.

"What are we supposed to do with this?" Peter asked, poking at the bread with his finger.

"Eat it! What do you think?" Jessica said, almost shouting.

Peter was about to say something rude when Dennis kicked him under the table. Jessica let out a big sigh and sat down. Four Sampson kids were definitely four too many. She had to figure out some way to make it through the afternoon.

Sploosh! A water balloon smacked against Elizabeth's arm.

"I guess you got me, Ken," she said to Ken Matthews, trying to be a good sport. She wiped her arm off with a towel and wrung out a corner of her T-shirt. When she looked up she saw Lila waving at her from the other side of the park. "I can't believe Jessica," Elizabeth muttered to herself. "This is the last time," she told Lila when she reached her booth.

"You should just keep the phone over by you," Lila said. "No one's called me all day. It's always Jessica—for you."

"The phone would drown over at my booth,"

Elizabeth said. She heard something like a shriek coming from the phone and quickly held it to her ear. "Jess? Is that you? Are you all right?"

Jessica's voice sounded almost like a sob. "No," she cried. "I'm not. It's a total disaster here. Every time I turn around another kid shows up. First it was just Susan and Dennis—then Peter—then Gretchen . . . now there're four . . ."

"You're kidding," Elizabeth said, suddenly sympathetic. "You mean all four kids are there now?"

"But it's even worse than that," Jessica continued, getting hysterical. "They're horrible, Lizzie. Every one of them is more trouble than a whole gang of normal kids. I wrecked the lunch—and they got into the living room—and . . ."

Elizabeth cut her off. Realizing now that Jessica wasn't kidding and really was in trouble, she decided it was time to help. "Have you tried being really strict with them?"

"I've tried everything," Jessica cried. "I just don't think I can hold out any longer. Can't you think of anything I can do before they destroy this whole house?"

Elizabeth thought fast. "You've got to scare them," she said. "You've got to get them to respect you, to listen to what you say."

Jessica snorted. "That's a joke. They wouldn't

even let me spread mustard on their sandwiches after I ruined the spaghetti."

Just then Patty Samuels, a sixth grader and a friend of Lila's, came up to the bottle-toss booth with her younger sisters—twins, dressed exactly alike, just the way Jessica and Elizabeth used to. Elizabeth brightened.

"Jess, I've got an idea," she exclaimed. "But I'm going to have to go home and get out of these sopping wet clothes first. Tell me what you're wearing."

"What I'm wearing! Have you gone crazy? What difference does it make?"

"Just tell me. And hurry. I'm going to have to see if I can get someone to take over the water-balloon booth so I can come help you." Elizabeth smirked. "And you know that could take me a while!"

"I'm wearing those designer jeans Mom got us at the mall last week—you know, the faded ones—and the navy and white striped T-shirt with the white collar." Once Jessica got started describing an outfit it was hard to stop her. "And my white tennis shoes—not the ankle ones, the low ones—and white socks with a navy stripe, and—"

"You don't have to tell me what kind of underwear you've got on," Elizabeth groaned.

"That's close enough. Is your hair down or in a ponytail?"

"Down," Jessica said quickly. Elizabeth heard something crash in the background and Jessica screamed "Stop that!" so loudly that Elizabeth almost dropped the phone. "Come quick," Jessica urged. "They're back in the living room and Peter's trying to watercolor the couch!"

"Hang on," Elizabeth said grimly. "I'll be there as fast as I can."

Eight

◇

Everywhere Jessica turned another Sampson kid was looking for trouble. Peter was stamping through the living room. Susan was twirling the dial on the TV in the family room. Dennis was trying to get another box of ice cream out of the freezer in the kitchen. Gretchen was trying out a survival skill she had learned in the Brownies that seemed to involve climbing all over the furniture.

"Stop it!" Jessica hollered at no one in particular.

"Telephone!" Susan screeched, snatching up the receiver. "Hi, Mommy!" she cried. "It's Mommy," she told everybody.

"Mommy! Mommy!" everyone started yelling. Jessica fought her way toward the phone just in time to hear Susan describing the spaghetti disaster.

"Let me talk to her," Jessica said.

She pulled the phone out of Susan's hand just in time to hear Mrs. Sampson say, "Well, we're calling from the cellular phone on the boat and can't stay on long, so I'm going to hang up. Be a good girl and help Jessica." And before Jessica could say a word she was gone.

Jessica felt like weeping.

"Mommy and Daddy are having a great time on the boat," Susan announced, turning back to the TV. Jessica groaned and retreated to the kitchen to try to calm herself down. She hoped Elizabeth got there fast.

Just then she heard a knock on the window and spun around, her eyes wide. She knew there weren't any more Sampson kids left—all four of them were already here. She raced to the window and looked out at her twin sister, standing in the rosebushes, tapping furiously on the window.

"Open it," Elizabeth mouthed.

Jessica opened the window and stared at her sister. It was like looking into a mirror. Elizabeth was wearing exactly what she was wearing, down to the last detail. The same jeans, the same striped T-shirt, even white tennis shoes.

"Where are they?" Elizabeth said, looking past her sister into the kitchen.

"In the living room, on a search-and-destroy mission," Jessica moaned. "Liz, you've got to help!"

"Why else do you think I'm standing in these rosebushes wearing exactly the same clothes as you?" Elizabeth demanded. "It's not for my entertainment."

Jessica shook her head. "Maybe I'm dumber than I thought, but I don't get it. What good is looking like me going to do?"

Elizabeth was trying to peer behind her into the kitchen. "You can't let them see me. Just take my word for it, Jess. We're going to get these kids to do exactly what we want them to do—I promise."

"How?"

"Just do what I tell you," Elizabeth commanded. "Get all four of them out into the yard—tell them anything, just get them outside."

"Then what?" Jessica demanded.

"Just keep them busy as long as you can. When things start to get bad I want you to tell them you're sick and tired of them and you're going back inside. Then announce where you're going, loud enough for me to hear. That's all you have to do."

Jessica shook her head. "I don't know, Lizzie. I mean, I want to think positively and everything, but you don't know what these kids are like." She couldn't help feeling disappointed. She had expected Elizabeth to have a great rescue plan and all she wanted was for Jessica to say something about going back inside the house!

"Just try it. You'll see," Elizabeth said, ducking as Gretchen approached the kitchen to look in the refrigerator.

Jessica stuck her head out the window. "Lizzie," she whispered. "Who'd you get to take over the water-balloon booth?"

Elizabeth laughed. "Lila," she said. "Everyone drew straws and she got stuck. She's pretty mad. She mentioned something about trying to get back at you—if you ever make it out of this place in one piece!"

"OK, you guys," Jessica said as she rounded up the four Sampson monsters and then gave them the sternest look she could muster. "We're all going outside and we're going to play kick the can together. It's way too nice a day for you to be cooped up in here."

She couldn't bear to look at the living room. Just a few hours ago this room had been in perfect condition. And now it looked like the rest of the house—like four Sampsons had torn it to pieces. Cushions were thrown everywhere. Books had been taken off shelves, a table was turned over, there were watercolor marks on the walls. *Mrs. Sampson is absolutely going to kill me*, Jessica thought sadly. *Lila is just going to have to wait in line.*

"I love kick the can," Peter exclaimed, leaping

to his feet. To Jessica's amazement his younger brother and his sisters traipsed after him through the kitchen out to the backyard. Jessica looked around frantically for Elizabeth, but she was nowhere to be found.

True to form, the gang of four promptly started a war about who was going to be on which side, who got to kick the can first, what to use instead of a can, and what the boundaries were. Jessica's patience had worn so thin she couldn't stand listening to them. When the actual fighting broke out, Jessica stood as tall as she could and cleared her throat loudly. *Elizabeth*, she thought, *I hope you're listening. And I hope this works, whatever it is.*

"I've had it," she said loudly. "I try to get you guys out here to play a nice civilized game and what do you do? You start pummeling each other. Well, I'm not watching another minute of this." She took a deep breath. "I'm going inside to the family room." She paused dramatically. "And not one of you had better follow me in there. I'm not kidding. I want to be alone. If *one* person tries to follow me there I'm going to be very angry!"

All four of the Sampson kids stared at her. Then Gretchen said to Peter, "Let's beat her there." And the next thing Jessica knew, they were flying across the lawn in front of her, running pell-mell toward the house. Jessica wrinkled her brow and charged after them. She didn't see the point of this. Did Elizabeth have the faintest idea of what she was doing?

She opened the back door and hurried through the kitchen just in time to hear Peter let out a bloodcurdling shriek. "How'd you do that? How'd you get in here so fast? We were in front of you," he cried.

Jessica dropped back behind the kitchen door and peered into the next room to see what was going on. There was Elizabeth, standing with her arms crossed. "I guess you're just not as fast as you think you are," she said in a loud clear voice.

Jessica stared. All four Sampson kids were gaping at Elizabeth, their mouths open and their eyes wide. "Didn't I tell you to leave me alone?" Elizabeth continued. "I'm going back outside to the tree house and I don't want you guys to follow me."

Jessica didn't wait to hear the Sampsons' protests. She knew that was her cue. Spinning on her heel, she tore back outside and across the yard to the tree house. When the gang of monsters came, she'd be ready for them!

"I am *so mad* at Jessica Wakefield," Lila seethed. She took a position gingerly behind the water-balloon table, staring miserably down at the expensive jumpsuit she was wearing. "This outfit had better not get wrecked!"

Amy and Julie giggled. Neither of them could believe Lila was now manning the water-balloon booth. Soon a big crowd had gathered to watch as Winston Egbert took aim. He held a big, slippery pink balloon.

"Duck, Lila!" everyone yelled.

But Lila didn't seem to have the timing right. The balloon hit her in the shoulder and water poured down her body. She sputtered, wiping away drops of water from her eyes.

"It's ruined! It's totally ruined!" she cried, staring down at the big water stain on her jumpsuit.

Amy couldn't hide her giggles. "It's only water, Lila," she pointed out.

But Lila's pride was injured and it was obvious to everyone that she wasn't going to be easy to calm down. "I can't wait to get my hands on that girl!" she muttered.

Nine

◇

Jessica was waiting by the tree house when the Sampson kids came charging across the lawn.

Peter stopped short, pointing at her and covering his mouth with his hand. "How—" he gasped.

Susan let out a cry. "No way," she hollered. "No way could you get out here before we did. You were behind us in the family room just a second ago."

Jessica just raised her eyebrows, enjoying their discomfort. Now that she realized what her twin's plan was she had to admit it was clever. She waited till she saw Elizabeth creep out and duck behind a bush, waiting for directions for the next destination in the game of baby-sitting tag. Then she cleared her throat. "You guys are just a bunch of slowpokes," she said disdainfully. "I bet I can make it to the basement in half the time it takes you."

"Bet you're wrong," Peter cried.

Jessica saw Elizabeth dart toward the house and distracted the kids by asking quickly, "If I beat you there, will you admit I've got magic powers?"

It was already too late. The Sampsons were scrambling across the lawn, turning their heads back to make sure Jessica was still behind them. She was really getting into this now. Holding her head high, she strolled calmly across the lawn, not even bothering to run. She waited till the basement door had slammed behind the last kid before tiptoeing forward, opening it noiselessly, and creeping down a few steps so she could see what was happening.

Elizabeth was sitting calmly on a bench in the basement, a satisfied smile on her face. "See, I told you," she said. "*Now* do you think I have magical powers?"

Susan started to cry and Gretchen bent down to comfort her.

"Do it again," Peter demanded, his eyes wide with admiration.

"I don't know if I feel like it," Elizabeth said.

"Come on, please!" everyone begged but Susan, who was still crying.

"OK. Beat you to the garage," Elizabeth cried.

Jessica leapt nimbly to her feet, dashed up the stairs, and scurried out to the garage. Then she clambered up onto one of the bicycles parked there and crossed her arms.

All four Sampson kids dashed through the garage door and lined up in front of Jessica. Expressions of complete awe washed over their faces. Jessica felt great and she had to fight back her laughter. For the first time all day she had them exactly where she wanted them. It wasn't a position she was willing to relinquish.

For the next twenty minutes she and Elizabeth played baby-sitting tag with the Sampson kids. They raced from room to room, up to the attic, out to the front yard, back to the basement, until the kids were worn out and completely mystified. Finally, Jessica was assured that her point had been made.

Elizabeth must have realized it, too. She winked at Jessica and waved from her spot behind the bushes. Then she slipped away quietly and Jessica was on her own again. But this time, it was going to be a lot easier.

"Tell us where you get your magic," Susan begged, wiping tears from her eyes. "Do you have spooky magic or good magic?"

"That depends," Jessica answered. "If you're good, my magic is good. If you're bad . . ." She let her voice trail off and Susan shrieked, covering her face with her hands.

"Promise you'll make your magic be good!" she cried.

Jessica gave her a stern look. "Only as long as *you* all promise to be good," she said solemnly. "You've all got to be good for the rest of the day and do what I tell you. OK?"

Everyone nodded solemnly. "Promise?" Jessica asked.

Susan wiped away the last tears. "We promise," she said, her eyes shining. "We've never had a magic baby-sitter before."

"I want to know where you get your magic from," Peter said skeptically. "Are you from an alien planet?"

"I can't tell you," Jessica said. "Just promise you're going to be good, or . . ." She gave them a scary look and Peter shivered.

"I promise," he said quickly.

"OK," Jessica said. "Now, I want you all to go back inside, and you can show me *your* magic."

"We can't do magic," Peter declared, staring at her.

"I bet you can," Jessica said. "For instance, I think you can transform the living room back to exactly how it looked before."

To her amazement, all four Sampson kids trotted back to the house. They were listening to her! Elizabeth's magic had really done the trick.

For a split second Jessica felt a pang of guilt. Elizabeth had really saved her life. What if she hadn't been there? What would have happened then?

But Jessica pushed the thought to the back of her mind. Now that the kids were behaving, she just wanted to relax and enjoy herself. After all, she had had a very hard day!

The rest of the afternoon was pure joy for Jessica. She couldn't believe the change in the Sampson kids' behavior. Every single one of them looked at her with a combination of fear and respect. They spent the first half-hour after Elizabeth left feverishly straightening the living room. Gretchen made a solution of soapy water to sponge the watercolors off the wall. Peter put the furniture back. Susan plumped the pillows and Dennis, much as he meant well, mostly just got in the way. Jessica couldn't believe it when she saw the results. The living room looked just as it did when the Sampsons had left that morning.

"Pretty good," Jessica said, trying to tone down her praise. *No sense letting them slide back into bad habits*, she thought.

"Wait a minute," Susan said, leading every-one out of the living room and holding up the key. "We need to lock it again so Mommy won't know—" She looked fearfully at Jessica. "So Mommy won't know we were bad."

"That's right," Jessica said cheerfully, watching with crossed arms. She wasn't any more eager than Susan was to tell Mrs. Sampson what a disaster area that living room had been just a short time earlier.

"Now," Jessica said sweetly, "should we surprise your parents by tidying up the other rooms, too, before we play a really fun game outside?"

She couldn't believe it when they obediently set about straightening up the family room and kitchen. *What a change*, she gloated. She had never seen four such good-tempered, well-behaved kids. It was nothing short of a miracle.

By the time the Sampsons got home at five o'clock, Jessica was so proud of herself as a baby-sitter that she had completely forgotten about the crisis earlier in the day.

"We're home!" Mrs. Sampson called, stepping into the front hall. "Jessica? Children? How's everything?"

"Mommy!" Susan squealed, racing out to fling her arms around her mother's legs. "Guess what? Jessica's a magic baby-sitter! She's been showing us all sorts of neat stuff she can do. And the best thing is, she knows how to be in two places at the same time!"

Mr. Sampson followed his wife into the family room. "Wait a minute," he said. "Am I seeing things or are there a few more of you here than there were this morning?"

Mrs. Sampson looked at Jessica with alarm. "You can't tell me all four children have been here all day!"

"Well, Peter came home first, I think," Jessica said slowly.

"Me and Joey got in a bad fight," Peter chirped.

"Peter," Mrs. Sampson said reproachfully. "You were Joey's guest today. I hope you didn't misbehave."

"Well, Joey started it!" Peter hung his head. "But I guess I sort of fought back a little bit. So I came home."

"We're going to have to talk about that later," Mrs. Sampson said, frowning at him. "And what about you?" She turned to Gretchen.

Gretchen explained that her troop leader had sprained her ankle and the hike was canceled. "But that's OK, Mom. It was *much* neater being here," she exclaimed. "If I'd known we were going to have a baby-sitter as cool as Jessica, I would've stayed home in the first place!"

"You mean to tell me that you took care of all four of these kids by yourself?" Mr. Sampson said incredulously, turning to stare at Jessica.

"She's magic, Daddy," Susan explained.

"She must be," Mr. Sampson marveled. "Jessica, this is miraculous! You've managed to keep four kids from destroying the place, and each other!"

"Can we always have Jessica for our baby-sitter from now on?" Dennis cried.

This suggestion was immediately seconded by the other Sampson kids.

"Well, if Jessica agrees to come back . . ." Mrs. Sampson said doubtfully.

Jessica made some kind of noncommittal noise. Actually, what she wanted more than anything was to pocket her seventy dollars, get out of there, and never come back. But she didn't think it would be polite to say so.

"She's the best baby-sitter ever," Gretchen gushed as Mrs. Sampson reached for her purse. "Pay her extra, Mama. Give her a big tip."

Jessica smiled widely at Gretchen. *What a nice girl*, she thought, reconsidering her reluctance ever to return.

"I think you deserve this," Mrs. Sampson said with a laugh, counting out eight ten-dollar bills. "Jessica, I mean it—you've done a wonderful job today. If you ever need a reference as a baby-sitter, you know who to ask."

Jessica smiled modestly. "Thanks," she said, delighted to take all the credit.

All in all, she thought things had worked out

pretty well. She'd made it through the day, she hadn't gotten water balloons dumped on her, and she had made eighty dollars—even more than she had expected! She could hardly wait to get home and figure out what to do with all that money.

Ten

◇

Elizabeth wasn't home from the fair when Jessica got back from the Sampsons' house. Mr. and Mrs. Wakefield were relaxing out in the backyard with Steven, who was lighting coals for the cookout they were having at dinnertime.

"Hi!" Jessica called, bouncing out to the backyard and giving each of her parents a kiss. "Hi, Godzilla," she said lightly to her older brother, who made a face at her.

"You're awfully cheerful. I take it baby-sitting went well," Mr. Wakefield said.

"Oh, it was fine," Jessica said casually, dropping down into a lounge chair and stretching out her legs. "You know how it is with kids." She shrugged modestly. "Once you know how to handle them . . ."

Steven snorted. "Yeah, and what do you know about handling little kids?" he demanded.

Jessica raised one eyebrow. "You may find this hard to believe, Steven, but the Sampsons said I was the best baby-sitter they've ever had."

Mrs. Wakefield looked surprised. "Darling, what a nice compliment!"

"That's quite a tribute to you, Jess," Mr. Wakefield agreed.

Jessica gave her brother a smug look. "You know what they say, 'either you have it or you don't.' " She giggled when Steven's third attempt to light the coals failed. "Like lighting a barbecue, right, Godzilla?"

"Quit calling me that," Steven grumbled.

Just then Jessica heard the screen door slam. "Oh, that must be Elizabeth," she said, scrambling out of the lounge chair. "I've . . . uh, I've got to talk to her about something." She wanted to catch Elizabeth alone before her twin said anything about the fiasco at the Sampsons' house, but Elizabeth was too quick for her. She was already stepping out onto the back patio.

"Hi, everyone," Elizabeth said, setting down her backpack. "Phew," she added, wiping her brow. "Nothing like a long day of getting pelted with water balloons to make you appreciate being dry for a change!"

Mrs. Wakefield frowned, studying her daughters' outfits. "Come over and tell us all about the fair," she said. "Did you two dress identically today on purpose or is this just some kind of coincidence?"

Jessica looked at her uneasily. Any minute now, Elizabeth was going to mention the Sampson kids and blow her story. "Liz, want to come inside for a sec?" she whispered.

Elizabeth shook her head. "I want to collapse, right out here in the sun," she said, sinking down in a chair between her parents. Only then did she really seem to acknowledge her sister's presence. "So," she said, looking Jessica up and down. "Looks like you survived the rest of the afternoon. Were the kids good after I left?"

Steven had finally managed to light the barbecue and stopped admiring the flames to listen to Elizabeth's question. "What are you talking about?" he demanded. "We've just been hearing how Jessica won the best-baby-sitter-in-history medal from the Sampsons."

Elizabeth laughed. Then her eyes widened as she began to get the idea. "Oh . . . really?" she said, her expression innocent. "They weren't any trouble at all?"

Jessica felt her cheeks turn red. "Well—I mean, they *did* think I was really great," she said hastily.

"*You* were great?" Elizabeth repeated incredulously.

Jessica really wished they could change the subject. "Well, yes, actually," she said. She inched closer to the patio door. "I've got to go upstairs and—"

"Wait a minute," Elizabeth exclaimed. "I want to hear all about your baby-sitting job, Jess. Don't stop now!"

But Jessica was much too embarrassed to go on. "I'm going upstairs," she blurted. "I'll be right back."

Elizabeth followed her inside. The minute the twins were alone Elizabeth really let her have it. "I guess as soon as things were under control you decided you could just drop me right out of your story," she said. She turned to her sister, shaking her head in disbelief. "I can't believe you, Jess. I knock myself out for you today and you try to pretend that you're the hero! Just remember, the next time you need help, you can count me out."

Jessica swallowed hard. "I was going to tell them the truth," she said. But Elizabeth wouldn't have any of it.

"Forget it," she snapped. "I'm going upstairs to change."

Dead silence followed Elizabeth's exit. Jessica stared down at the ground, feeling absolutely terrible. She knew Elizabeth was right. And she knew she was going to have to do whatever she could to make her twin see she knew she'd messed up.

*   *   *

Jessica knocked softly on Elizabeth's door later that night. "Lizzie? Can I come in?"

"Uh, just a second. I'm on the phone," Elizabeth said hastily. Jessica could hear her saying goodbye to someone and then she heard her say, "Yeah, I think it'll be really funny. What a great idea."

"What's a great idea?" Jessica demanded, stepping into her sister's bedroom.

"Oh, nothing," Elizabeth said casually. "What's up?"

Jessica sat down on the edge of her bed. "I know you're mad at me. And I know I shouldn't have told Mom and Dad that I was the one who was a great baby-sitter. So I just want to tell you I'm really sorry and thanks for all your help today." She took a deep breath. This was much more painful than she'd thought it would be.

Elizabeth looked at her. "So," she said, after a pause. "I guess the Sampsons paid you a lot, huh?"

"Eighty dollars," Jessica said triumphantly. "Ten dollars an hour. Plus a ten dollar tip."

Elizabeth looked at her expectantly. "How much did you say, Jess?"

"Ummm . . . forty dollars," Jessica corrected herself.

She reached into her pocket and dug out a

fistful of bills. "I guess I don't really deserve all of this." She counted out four ten-dollar bills and gave them to Elizabeth.

Elizabeth looked thoughtfully at the money. "You keep the tip and just give me thirty," she said judiciously, putting thirty dollars on her nightstand. "And thanks, Jess."

Jessica stared at her feet. "I really couldn't have done it without you, Lizzie. And I'm sorry I stole your job in the first place and stuck you with the water-balloon booth and everything."

"Oh, that's OK, Jess," Elizabeth said slowly, fiddling with the edge of her bedspread. "I'm sorry you had to miss such a great time today. Let's go downstairs and tell Mom and Dad all about the fair and the money we raised for the class fund!"

Amy Sutton called Jessica that evening after dinner. "You sure were a hit with the Sampsons, Jessica. I don't know what you did, but all four of them were going on and on about what a great baby-sitter you were. Mrs. Sampson called to see if I'd mind if she asked you to baby-sit sometimes, too. She said the kids would be too disappointed if you never came back."

"Oh, well," Jessica said. "I don't think I'm really cut out to be a baby-sitter, Amy. I mean, if Mrs. Sampson really wants me to, I guess I could every once in a while. But she's got so many kids!"

"I know." Amy giggled. "They can be a handful. Well, the other reason I was calling is that some of us are trying to set up a mini-fair after school on Monday. We all felt so bad about you missing today's fair that we thought it would be fun to show you what it was like."

"That's awfully nice, Amy. But you don't have to do that," Jessica said. "I'm sure I can get enough of an idea just from listening to what all of you guys say about it and stuff."

"But we want to do it, Jessica," Amy insisted. "It's all set up. Monday, at the parkground, as soon as school gets out."

Jessica bit her lip. "Well, if you really want to," she said doubtfully.

"Oh, we do!" Amy said cheerfully. "We really do." She paused for a minute. "Oh, and thanks again for taking over for me today. You did a wonderful job."

"It was nothing," Jessica said.

When she hung up the phone, she got a bad feeling about Monday afternoon.

Jessica ran down the hall to her sister's room and burst in without knocking. "Lizzie, tell me what's going on with this mini-fair thing," she demanded. "Amy sounded mysterious about it on the phone."

Elizabeth looked up from the novel she was reading and raised her eyebrows. "Oh, it's nothing, Jess. Just a chance to get together and have fun," she said.

Jessica's eyes sparkled. "Good!" she said. And once again she had to remind herself how lucky she was. She had come out of this day fifty dollars richer—and now she wouldn't have to feel bad about missing the fair!

Eleven

"This is going to be great, don't you think?" Lila asked Ellen Riteman. It was Monday after school and Lila and Ellen were walking with Jessica to the park for their very own mini-fair.

"Yeah," Ellen said, her eyes shining. "I think it's amazing that people felt so bad about Jessica missing the fair that they're all willing to have a rerun."

"Yeah," Jessica said. "It is." She was really looking forward to this. It made her feel good inside to think she was so important to her friends.

Elizabeth, Julie, and Amy had gotten to the park before them, and a small group of sixth graders had come along, too—Ken Matthews, Caroline Pearce, and a couple of sixth-grade girls in the Unicorn Club. As they approached, Jessica could see that everyone was crowded around a table. When Amy Sutton turned around, Jessica let out a cry. Amy was holding a big, fat water balloon!

"We felt sorry for you, missing out on running the water-balloon booth and everything," Julie said with a big grin.

"Yeah," Lila said. "I didn't realize it until I had to take over for Elizabeth, Jess. But it really is a lot of fun. We felt just awful, knowing you'd given it up for that long, hard day of baby-sitting."

Jessica could see she was stuck. There was no way out. "I guess telling you I'm really sorry wouldn't quite be the same thing, huh?" she demanded as Ellen and Julie led her to the target spot behind the table.

"I don't know about anyone else, but I just couldn't live with the guilt," Lila crowed. "After getting one of my very best outfits totally ruined on Saturday, I know I'd never be able to look at it again without thinking what a *shame* it was Jessica never got a chance to do this. You know what I mean?"

"OK, OK," Jessica grumbled. "Go ahead and fire."

Lila took the first shot and she missed. The balloon sailed right past Jessica and splattered on the grass.

Everyone applauded. "Well done, Jess!" Ken Matthews hollered.

Amy was next. Her balloon missed, too. It hit the edge of the table and exploded, spraying Winston and Ken, who both jumped backwards, yelping as the cold water hit them.

"Your turn next, Elizabeth," Amy said, handing her a slippery purple balloon.

Elizabeth slid the balloon from one hand to the other, taking her time. After a long pause, she flung it as hard as she could. It hit Jessica squarely on the shoulder and shattered, drenching her whole upper body.

The whole crowd burst into wild applause.

Jessica was sputtering with anger as she wiped the water from her arms and face. She was all set to scream at her twin but her fury melted when she looked around at all her friends and realized how ridiculous the situation was. She started to giggle instead.

"OK," she said good-naturedly, "you got me. Now can we cut this out and go do something fun—like go to the beach?"

"Sounds good. Then you can dry out," Amy said with a laugh.

Soon the whole group was heading for the beach. Ken had the good idea of bringing a few water balloons in case anyone got hot!

*   *   *

"Well, isn't it nice to see my children arguing again," Mrs. Wakefield commented later that evening, watching the twins fight over the remote control for the TV. "I was wondering why everyone around here was getting along so well!"

Jessica laughed. "We're just fooling around, Mom." She gave Elizabeth a little smile.

"Oh, by the way," Mrs. Wakefield said. "Mrs. Sampson called. She wanted to know if you want to baby-sit again this Saturday, Jessica."

Jessica dissolved into giggles. "Nah. I think I'll let Lizzie do it."

"Nah . . ." Elizabeth mimicked. "I think I'll let you do it again, Jess. After all, you had so much fun last time."

Both twins cracked up. "I think Mrs. Sampson is going to have to go back to using Amy Sutton," Jessica told her mother. "My baby-sitting career is on hold for now. And besides, I have to go shopping on Saturday. I have to figure out what to do with all that money I made."

"Well, call her back and let her know," Mrs. Wakefield said.

Secretly, Jessica thought about how well she had come out of the whole disaster. One water balloon wasn't as bad as a whole day of them. And now that Saturday was safely in the past and she was fifty dollars richer, she didn't even think she would mind seeing the Sampson kids again.

A few days after Jessica's private water-balloon toss, Mr. Bowman made a special announcement in English class. Jessica was sitting with Ellen, Elizabeth, and Amy in the back of the room when he pulled a map down and pointed at a tiny speck of land on the Mediterranean coast between Spain and France.

"See this country? Can anyone tell me what it's called?" he asked.

Amy leaned over to whisper to Elizabeth. "Mr. Bowman's wearing weirder clothes than usual today," she said with a giggle. The English teacher was famous for his mismatched outfits and that day his striped shirt and plaid pants were no exception.

Mr. Bowman cleared his throat. "Amy, can you tell us the name of this country?"

Amy squinted at the map. "I don't know, Mr. Bowman," she admitted.

Mr. Bowman turned to the rest of the class. "Does anyone else know?"

No one did.

"This country is a principality—a very small country with its own government. It's called Santa Dora. And for the next three weeks we're going to be studying its literature. In history, you'll learn the history of the country. And in art class, you'll learn about its native folk art. For three weeks the entire sixth grade is doing an intensive study of the country. We're hoping that by learning about it from all these angles, you'll have a sense of the cultural diversity of different nations." He looked very pleased. "We're even going to do a few classes on the music of Santa Dora."

Jessica rolled her eyes. But Elizabeth and Amy both looked interested.

"How big is the country?" Elizabeth asked.

"Not very big. The entire population is only a little bit larger than Sweet Valley."

"A whole country with a population the size of Sweet Valley?" Jessica couldn't believe it.

Mr. Bowman nodded. "We'll be learning much more about this country over the next several weeks."

Elizabeth and Amy smiled at each other. They both thought this project sounded like fun.

When the bell rang, everyone filed out, still talking about Santa Dora.

"Who cares about such a dinky little country, anyway?" Jessica complained. "It's not even famous for anything."

"Oh, Jess, it'll be exciting to learn about someplace so different," Elizabeth said, trying to persuade her twin.

"You know what I heard?" Caroline Pearce said. "There's an exchange student coming here the week after next from Santa Dora. That's one of the reasons we're studying it."

"You're kidding!" Elizabeth's eyes were shining. She thought Santa Dora sounded magical. It would be great to meet someone who actually lived there.

"I overheard Mr. Bowman talking about it with one of the other teachers," Caroline went on. "Supposedly they're going to make a big announcement on Monday."

Jessica didn't look very interested. She was fussing with the lace on her tennis shoe when Caroline added, "And it's a boy. I couldn't hear what his name was, but it was definitely a he they were talking about."

Suddenly Jessica perked up. A *boy*—from this romantic, exotic country—coming to Sweet Valley to study with them? She couldn't believe it. This *was* something to be excited about!

She pumped Caroline for more information, but Caroline insisted she had told her all she knew.

"We'll just have to wait till Monday to find out more."

Jessica's eyes were sparkling. She knew one thing. She wanted to be one of the first people to meet the new exchange student and find out everything she possibly could about him.

She had no idea how she was going to wait until Monday to find out more!

What will the boy from Santa Dora be like? Find out in Sweet Valley Twins #30, **PRINCESS ELIZABETH.**

YOUR OWN

SLAM BOOK!

If you've read *Slambook Fever*, Sweet Valley High #48, you know that slam books are the rage at Sweet Valley High. Now *you* can have a slam book of your own! Make up your own categories, such as "Biggest Jock" or "Best Looking," and have your friends fill in the rest! There's a four-page calendar, horoscopes and questions most asked by Sweet Valley readers with answers from Elizabeth and Jessica.

It's a must for SWEET VALLEY fans!

☐ **05496 FRANCINE PASCAL'S SWEET VALLEY HIGH SLAM BOOK**
Laurie Pascal Wenk $3.95

SWEET VALLEY TWINS

Buy them at your local bookstore or use this handy page for ordering:

Bantam Books, Dept. SVT3, 414 East Golf Road, Des Plaines, IL 60016

Please send me the items I have checked above. I am enclosing $_____
(please add $2.00 to cover postage and handling). Send check or money
order, no cash or C.O.D.s please.

Mr/Ms _____

Address _____

City/State_____Zip_____

Please allow four to six weeks for delivery.   SVT3-9/89
Prices and availability subject to change without notice.